MAY - 2004

DISCARD
FCPL discards materials that are outdated
and in poor condition. In order to make room
for current, in-demand materials, underused
materials are offered for public sale.

In the Kitchen

Let's Make Cookies

By Mary Hill

Children's Press®
A Division of Scholastic Inc.
New York / Toronto / London / Auckland / Sydney
Mexico City / New Delhi / Hong Kong
Danbury, Connecticut

Photo Credits: Cover and all photos by Maura B. McConnell
Contributing Editor: Jennifer Silate
Book Design: Mindy Liu

Library of Congress Cataloging-in-Publication Data

Hill, Mary, 1977-
Let's make cookies / by Mary Hill.
   p. cm. — (In the kitchen)
Includes index.
Summary: Simple text and photographs depict a young boy and his father making chocolate chip cookies.
ISBN 0-516-23958-9 (lib. bdg.) — ISBN 0-516-24019-6 (pbk.)
 1. Cookies—Juvenile literature. [1. Chocolate chip cookies. 2. Cookies. 3. Baking.] I. Title.

TX772 .H553 2002
641.8'654--dc21

2002004868

Copyright © 2002 by Rosen Book Works, Inc.
All rights reserved. Published simultaneously in Canada.
Printed in the United States of America.
1 2 3 4 5 6 7 8 9 10 R 11 10 09 08 07 06 05 04 03 02

Contents

1. Chocolate Chip Cookies   4
2. Making the Dough   6
3. Into the Oven   18
4. New Words   22
5. To Find Out More   23
6. Index   24
7. About the Author   24

Hello, my name is David.

Dad and I are going to make **chocolate chip** cookies.

First, we make the cookie **dough**.

I put some **flour** in a bowl.

Dad adds **baking powder** and salt.

I **stir** everything together.

9

We put the eggs, butter, and sugar in another bowl.

We use both brown sugar and white sugar.

Next, Dad uses the **egg beater** to mix everything together.

I put some of the flour **mixture** into this bowl.

13

Now, I add the chocolate chips.

I put in a lot!

Next, I use a spoon to put the dough on a **cookie sheet**.

The cookie sheet is full.

Dad puts it into the hot oven.

The cookies are done.

They must cool before we can eat them.

I cannot wait!

New Words

baking powder (**bayk**-ing **pou**-dur) a white powder used to make dough rise

chocolate chip (**chok**-lit **chip**) candy made from the beans of the cacao tree

cookie sheet (**kuk**-ee **sheet**) a tray used for baking cookies

dough (**doh**) a soft, sticky mixture of flour, water, and other things, used to make bread, cookies, muffins, and other food

egg beater (**eg beet**-ur) a machine that is used to stir something quickly

flour (**flou**-ur) a fine powder made by grinding and sifting a grain

mixture (**miks**-chur) something that has different things mixed together

stir (**stur**) to mix things by moving them around with a spoon

To Find Out More

Books
Alphabake: A Cookbook and Cookie Cutter Set
by Debora Pearson
Dutton Children's Books

Rookie Cookie Cookbook
by Betty Debnam
Random House Value Publishing

Web Site
KidsHealth For Kids
http://kidshealth.org/kid/stay_healthy/recipe_links.html
This Web site has lots of different recipes to try.

Index

baking powder, 8

chocolate chips, 14

cookie sheet, 16, 18

dough, 6, 16

egg beater, 12

flour, 6, 12

mixture, 12

oven, 18

About the Author

Mary Hill writes and edits children's books from her home in Maryland.

Reading Consultants

Kris Flynn, Coordinator, Small School District Literacy, The San Diego County Office of Education

Shelly Forys, Certified Reading Recovery Specialist, W.J. Zahnow Elementary School, Waterloo, IL

Sue McAdams, Former President of the North Texas Reading Council of the IRA, and Early Literacy Consultant, Dallas, TX